PATTERN FISH

Trudy Harris

illustrations by Anne Canevari Green

Ⓜ MILLBROOK PRESS • MINNEAPOLIS

Yellow-black.
Yellow-black.
A fish swims in the ocean.
It has stripes upon its back.
Yellow-black, yellow-black, yellow . . .

black.

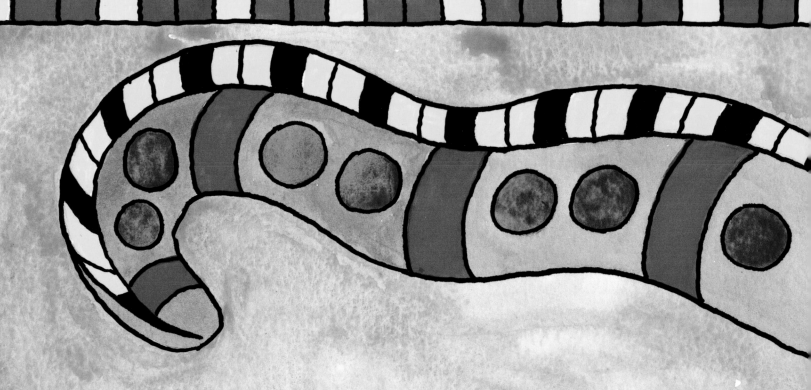

Stripe-dot-dot,
Stripe-dot-dot.
From a dark and rocky nook
An eel slips out to take a look.
Stripe-dot-dot, stripe-dot-dot, stripe-dot . . .

d.o.t.

Chomp-chomp-munch-munch,
Chomp-chomp-munch-munch.
A sea horse, underneath the sea,
Eats seaweed for its lunch.
Chomp-chomp-munch-munch, chomp-chomp-munch-munch,
chomp-chomp-munch . . .

munch.

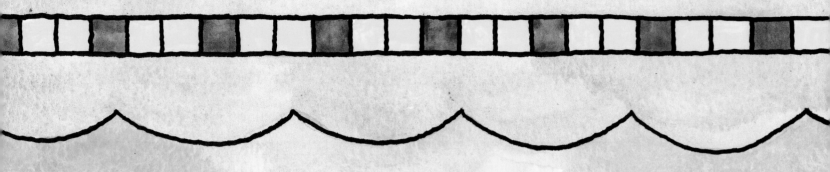

Bubble-bubble-pop,
Bubble-bubble-pop.
A puffer fish blows bubbles.
They go floating to the top.
Bubble-bubble-pop, bubble-bubble-pop, bubble-bubble . . .

pop.

Stretch-spurt-glide,
Stretch-spurt-glide.
On an underwater ride
An octopus is slowly going
Stretch-spurt-glide, stretch-spurt-glide, stretch-spurt . . .

g l

ide.

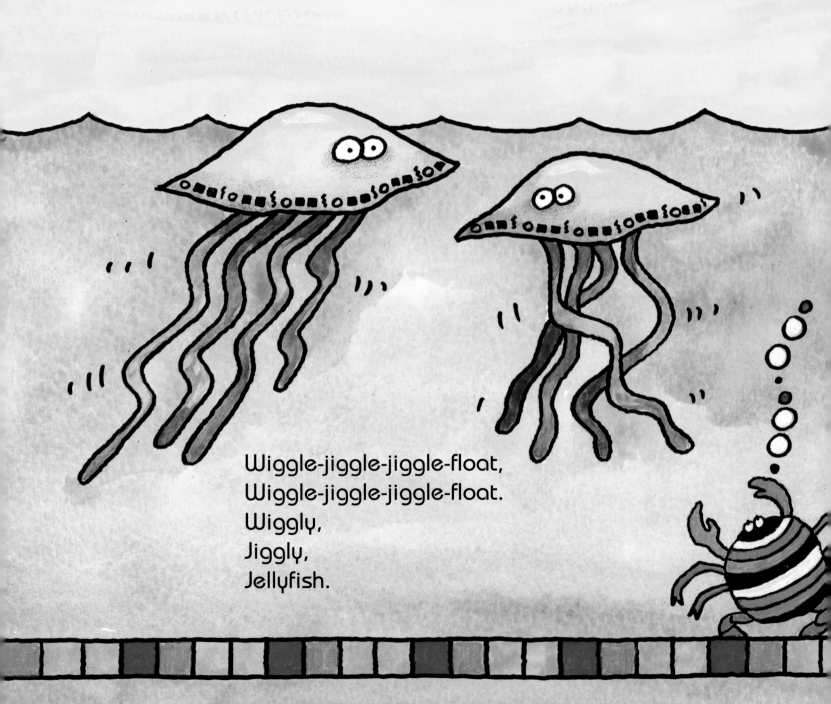

Wiggle-jiggle-jiggle-float,
Wiggle-jiggle-jiggle-float.
Wiggly,
Jiggly,
Jellyfish.

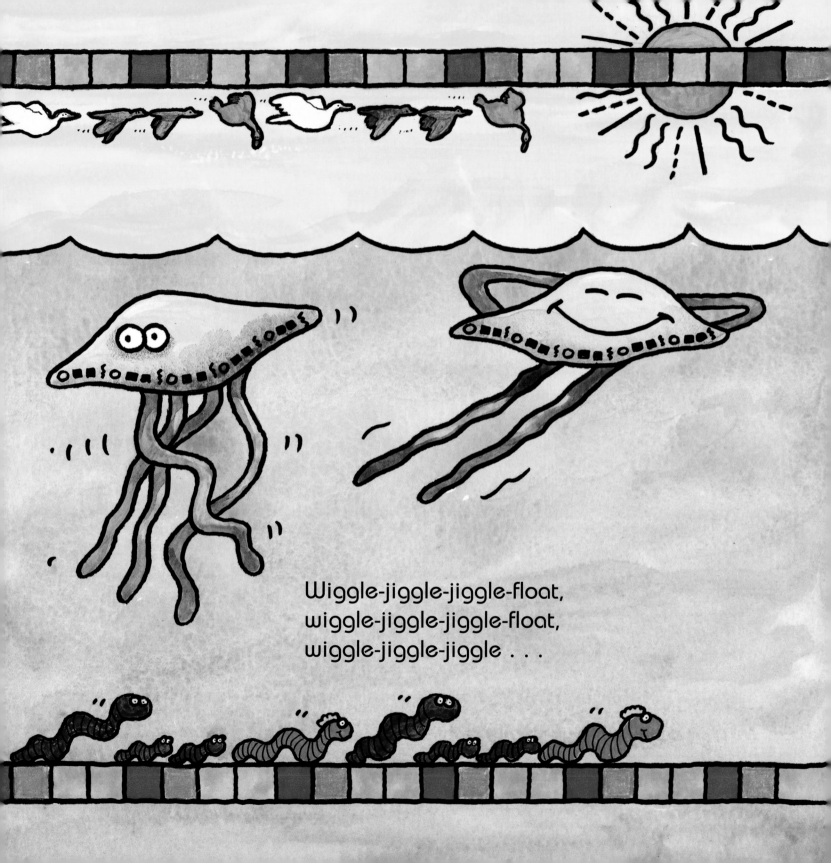

Wiggle-jiggle-jiggle-float,
wiggle-jiggle-jiggle-float,
wiggle-jiggle-jiggle . . .

float.

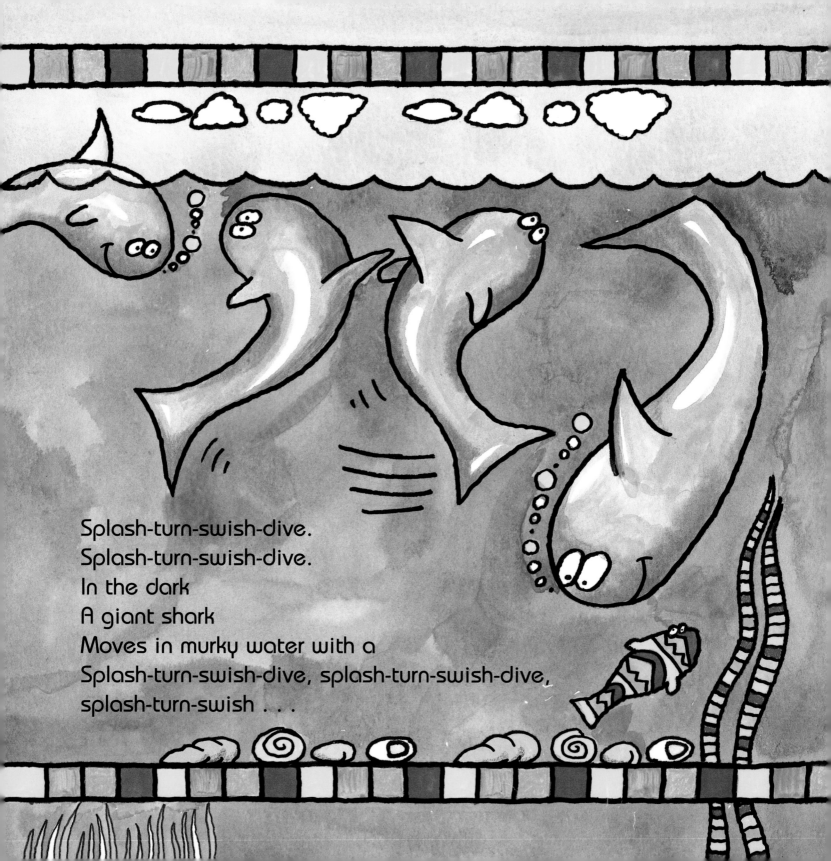

Splash-turn-swish-dive.
Splash-turn-swish-dive.
In the dark
A giant shark
Moves in murky water with a
Splash-turn-swish-dive, splash-turn-swish-dive,
splash-turn-swish . . .

Shark?
Shark?

Yellow-black, yellow-black!

Stripe-dot-dot, stripe-dot-dot!

Chomp-chomp-munch-munch!

"Hey, where did everybody go?"
"Oh, well."
Splash-turn-swish-dive, splash-turn-swish-dive, splash-turn-swish . . .

ABOUT PATTERNS

A pattern is something that repeats again and again. An AB pattern has only two different things that repeat over and over.

This is an AAB pattern because the "A" picture appears two times before the "B" picture.

In an ABB pattern, the "A" part is followed by two "B's." Colors make up this example of an ABB pattern.

An ABC pattern always has three different things in it. This is an ABC pattern.

Some patterns are heard, not seen. When a clock goes "tick-tock, tick-tock, tick-tock," it is making an AB sound pattern. A bell's "ding-dong, ding-dong, ding-dong" is also an AB pattern. The "oom-pa-pa, oom-pa-pa" of a tuba is an ABB pattern.

AND NOW THE TREASURE HUNT

Look at the frame around the first spread of each pattern. The pattern of the frame tells you what pattern to look for in the art. Every picture has elements that match the pattern in the picture's frame.

Look at the first picture. This frame has an AB pattern because there are only two colors that repeat—green and pink. Can you find an AB pattern in the picture that goes "little-big, little-big"? How about one that goes "red-pink, red-pink"? There are more AB patterns in the picture for you to find.

On the same page, the words "yellow-black, yellow-black" make another AB pattern. When we say them aloud, these words form a sound pattern. Patterns are fun to hear, fun to see, and fun to find, so let the pattern hunt begin!